Jake's Shadowed Truths

Jake's Shadowed Truths

A Tale of Trust, Love, and Lies

Anurag Anurag

Anurag Anurag

CONTENTS

CONTENTS

A Glimpse of Destiny

The grand hall of the reception was abuzz with laughter and music. Guests, dressed in their finest attire, mingled and danced under the glittering chandeliers. Among them was Jake, a young criminal lawyer known for his sharp mind and quick wit. He stood near the bar, nursing a glass of wine, his eyes scanning the room with mild interest.

As he took a sip, his gaze locked onto a woman across the room. She was stunning, with dark hair cascading in waves over her shoulders, her elegant dress hugging her figure perfectly. Their eyes met, and in that instant, it was as if the world around them faded away. She smiled softly, a gesture that sent a thrill down his spine.

Jake's friend, Mark, approached, noticing his friend's distraction. "Hey, Jake! You look like you've seen a ghost," he teased, clapping Jake on the back.

Jake blinked, snapping back to reality. "You see that girl over there?" he nodded towards her direction. "I feel like I know her, but I don't."

Mark followed his gaze and grinned. "She's gorgeous, man. Why don't you go talk to her?"

"Yeah, I think I will," Jake replied, setting down his glass and straightening his tie.

Just as he started to make his way towards her, another friend, Susan, intercepted him. "Jake! Come on, you promised me a dance," she insisted, dragging him towards the dance floor.

Jake cast a longing glance back at the woman, but Susan was relentless. "Alright, alright," he chuckled, "but just one dance."

As they danced, Jake kept trying to catch a glimpse of the mysterious woman. After the song ended, he excused himself and hurried back to where he had last seen her. But she was gone.

Panicking slightly, he began to search the reception hall, weaving through the crowd, looking for her familiar face. He approached a group of people near where she had been standing.

"Excuse me," he said, trying to keep his voice steady, "there was a woman here, dark hair, blue dress. Do any of you know who she is?"

The group exchanged glances and shrugged. "Sorry, mate," one of them said, "we haven't seen anyone like that."

Jake's heart sank. He moved from one group to another, repeating his question, but no one had seen her. It was as if she had vanished into thin air.

Feeling defeated, Jake returned to the bar. Mark was there, finishing his drink. "No luck, huh?" he asked sympathetically.

Jake shook his head. "It's like she just disappeared. I can't stop thinking about her, though. It felt... different."

Mark gave him a pat on the back. "Maybe it's just not meant to be tonight. But hey, if it's meant to be, you'll see her again."

Jake sighed, staring into his empty glass. "Yeah, maybe."

The reception continued, but Jake's mind was elsewhere. He couldn't shake the image of her smile, the way her eyes had sparkled when they met his. Eventually, the night ended, and Jake found himself walking home alone, his thoughts consumed by the mystery woman.

As he lay in bed that night, he replayed the brief encounter over and over in his mind. Who was she? Why had she disappeared so suddenly? He vowed that if he ever saw her again, he wouldn't let the opportunity slip away. With that thought, he drifted into a restless sleep, dreaming of the woman who had captured his heart in a fleeting moment.

The Unexpected Reunion

Six months had passed since the night of the wedding reception, yet Jake couldn't get the mysterious woman out of his mind. His days were busy with cases and courtrooms, but his thoughts often drifted back to her. It was during one of these daydreams that he found himself at the airport, waiting for a flight to Rome for a business trip.

As he navigated through the bustling terminal, his heart nearly stopped when he spotted her. There she was, the same captivating woman, standing near a café, looking at the flight schedule. Jake couldn't believe his luck. He felt a rush of adrenaline as he approached her.

"Excuse me," he said, hoping he didn't sound too eager. "I couldn't help but notice you. Weren't you at a wedding reception a few months ago?"

She turned to him, her eyes widening in recognition. "Yes, I was," she replied, her voice as enchanting as he remembered. "You look familiar. Were you there too?"

"I was," he nodded, a smile spreading across his face. "I'm Jake. We made eye contact, but then I lost you in the crowd."

Her face lit up with a smile. "I remember now. I'm Emily. I had to leave early that night. It's so strange running into you here."

"Very strange, but a good kind of strange," Jake chuckled. "Are you headed to Rome too?"

"Yes, for a business trip," she said. "And you?"

"Same here," he replied. "What a coincidence. Maybe we can catch up while we're there?"

"I'd like that," Emily said. "I have a business seat. What about you?"

"Main cabin," Jake admitted with a shrug. "But let's exchange numbers. I'd love to meet up in Rome."

They exchanged phone numbers and spent the next half hour chatting about their lives and work. The more they talked, the more Jake found himself drawn to her. She was intelligent, funny, and shared many of his interests. He couldn't believe his luck.

When it was time to board, they parted ways with a promise to meet up in Rome. Jake took his seat in the main cabin, his mind racing with excitement about the days ahead.

The flight seemed to drag on forever. He tried to sleep but couldn't stop thinking about Emily. When the plane finally landed in Rome, he quickly gathered his things and rushed out, hoping to find her. But as he scanned the crowd at the baggage claim, she was nowhere to be seen.

He pulled out his phone and called her number. It rang and rang, but there was no answer. Frowning, he sent her a text message: "Hey Emily, it's Jake. Just landed. Where are you?"

No response. He tried calling again, but still no answer. Puzzled, Jake waited for a while at the baggage claim, hoping she would appear. After about an hour, he reluctantly left, assuming she had gone ahead to her hotel.

Over the next few days, Jake called and texted repeatedly, but there was no response from Emily. His initial excitement turned into concern. What if something had happened to her? He visited the places they had planned to meet, but she never showed up.

Eventually, Jake had to return home, deeply disappointed and confused. Back in his town, he couldn't stop thinking about Emily and why she hadn't picked up the phone. Was it something he had said or done? Or was there another reason?

Days turned into weeks, and he still couldn't shake off the memory of their brief reunion. He kept her number saved, hoping that one day she might reach out and explain. Until then, all he could do was wonder about the mysterious woman who had come into his life, only to disappear once again.

Blossoming Love

Over the next few months, Jake and Emily's relationship blossomed. Their time together, though sporadic, was filled with joy and a growing sense of connection. They met occasionally, spending weekends together whenever their schedules allowed. Each encounter deepened their bond, and Jake found himself falling for her more with each passing day.

One sunny Friday afternoon, Jake and Emily decided to escape the city's hustle and bustle and retreat to a quaint countryside inn. The drive was picturesque, with rolling hills and lush greenery stretching as far as the eye could see. They chatted about everything and nothing, laughing and enjoying each other's company.

Upon arriving at the inn, they were greeted by the warm, rustic charm of the place. The innkeeper showed them to their cozy room, complete with a fireplace and a view of the sprawling gardens outside. Jake felt a sense of contentment he hadn't known in years.

The next morning, they decided to explore the inn's beautiful gardens. As they walked hand-in-hand through the lush, fragrant paths, Jake couldn't help but feel that everything was perfect. Birds sang in the trees, and a gentle breeze rustled the leaves.

"Jake," Emily said suddenly, her voice soft. She stopped walking and turned to face him.

Jake noticed the serious expression on her face and felt a hint of worry. "What is it?" he asked, gently squeezing her hand.

"I have to tell you something," Emily began, her gaze fixed on the rippling water of a nearby lake. "I work for an import-export business."

Jake nodded, waiting for her to continue.

"I travel a lot," she said, her eyes meeting his. "And sometimes I can't talk because of connectivity issues and different time zones."

Jake felt a wave of relief. He had feared something worse. "I understand," he said, taking both of her hands in his. "It must be challenging."

"It is," Emily admitted, her expression softening. "But I want you to know that I'm always thinking about you, even when we can't talk."

Jake smiled, pulling her into a gentle embrace. "I believe you, Emily. And I'll wait for you, no matter what."

Emily's eyes shimmered with gratitude. "Thank you, Jake. That means more to me than you know."

Their weekends together became a cherished routine, filled with adventures and quiet moments alike. They explored new places, shared stories, and grew closer with each passing day. Each parting became more difficult than the last, but Jake's faith in their relationship never wavered. He believed in Emily and the love they shared.

On Sundays, when it was time for Emily to leave for her next trip, Jake would walk her to her car, holding her close for as long as possible. "Stay safe," he would whisper, kissing her forehead.

"I will," she would reply, her eyes reflecting the same longing and promise of return.

As Jake watched her drive away each time, he felt a mix of pride and sorrow. Pride in the strong, independent woman he had fallen for, and sorrow at the inevitable separation. But he knew they were building something special, and that thought carried him through the days and weeks until they could be together again.

Despite the challenges of her job, Jake remained steadfast in his support. He learned to cherish the moments they had, understanding that love sometimes meant enduring the difficulties of time and distance. Their bond grew stronger, rooted in trust and the unwavering belief that their love was worth every sacrifice.

4

A Shocking Revelation

Months passed, and Jake adjusted to Emily's sporadic presence in his life. They had settled into a routine of weekend getaways and cherished moments whenever their schedules aligned. Each parting was difficult, but their reunions made the wait worthwhile. Jake's faith in their relationship remained unwavering, strengthened by the love they shared.

One evening, Jake returned home from a long day at the office. He poured himself a glass of wine and settled on the couch, flipping on the TV to catch the evening news. The usual headlines flashed across the screen: politics, sports, local events. Jake's mind wandered to thoughts of Emily and their plans for the next weekend.

Suddenly, the news anchor's voice drew his attention. "Breaking news," she announced, her tone grave. "The FBI has named a new addition to their Most Wanted list. An individual suspected of being a German spy involved in international espionage. The suspect is known by the alias Emily."

Jake's heart stopped. His eyes widened in disbelief as a photograph of Emily appeared on the screen, her name and details scrolling beneath it. The room seemed to spin, and Jake struggled to process what he was hearing. It felt as though the ground had been ripped out from under him.

"No, this can't be true," he whispered to himself, staring at the screen. His mind raced with confusion and disbelief. How could the woman he loved be involved in something so dangerous and deceitful?

His phone buzzed, snapping him out of his daze. It was a call from an unknown number. Jake hesitated for a moment before answering, his hand trembling.

"Hello?" he said, his voice barely above a whisper.

"Mr. Jake, this is Agent Collins with the FBI. We need to talk to you about Emily."

Jake swallowed hard, trying to steady his voice. "What is this about? Emily is not a spy."

"Mr. Jake, we understand this is difficult for you," Agent Collins said, his tone professional yet empathetic. "But we need your cooperation. Emily has been under investigation for a while now. We believe she may have used you to gain access to certain information."

Jake's mind reeled. Used him? How could that be possible? "I don't believe it," he said, his voice rising. "Emily wouldn't do that."

"We understand your loyalty to her, but we have substantial evidence linking her to espionage activities," Agent Collins continued. "We need to know everything you can tell us about her."

Jake felt a mix of anger, fear, and betrayal. "I'll cooperate," he said finally, his voice hollow. "But I need to understand what's happening."

"Thank you, Mr. Jake," Agent Collins replied. "We'll send someone to meet with you shortly. Please gather any information or documents you have related to Emily."

Jake hung up the phone, his hands shaking. He sank back onto the couch, staring blankly at the television screen. The news continued to report on Emily, showing images of her and listing the alleged crimes she was involved in. Each word felt like a dagger to his heart.

How could he have been so blind? How could he not have seen the signs? The love of his life was now a wanted criminal, and he was caught in the middle of a nightmare. Jake buried his face in his hands, trying to make sense of the chaos that had suddenly engulfed his life.

The knock on his door came an hour later. Jake opened it to find two FBI agents standing there, their expressions serious. "Mr. Jake, we're here to take your statement," one of them said.

Jake nodded numbly, stepping aside to let them in. As he began recounting everything he knew about Emily, he felt a sense of surreal detachment. The woman he loved, the woman he believed in, was not who she claimed to be. And now, he was left to pick up the pieces of a shattered reality.

5

Under Investigation

Jake found himself in a sterile interrogation room at the FBI headquarters, facing a panel of stern-faced agents. The room was stark, with white walls and a single table surrounded by uncomfortable chairs. The fluorescent lights overhead cast a harsh glare, amplifying Jake's sense of unease.

"Mr. Jake, how long have you known Emily?" Agent Collins asked, his tone professional but probing.

"About a year," Jake replied, his voice steady despite the turmoil inside him.

Agent Collins leaned forward, scrutinizing Jake's expression. "Did she ever mention her work or any suspicious activities?" another agent probed, tapping a pen against his notepad.

Jake took a deep breath, trying to maintain his composure. "She told me she worked in import-export and traveled a lot," he explained.

The agents exchanged glances before continuing their line of questioning. "Did you ever notice anything unusual about her behavior? Any strange communications or unexplained absences?"

Jake shook his head. "No, nothing that seemed out of the ordinary. She was always upfront about her travels. We spent as much time together as we could."

Agent Collins continued, his voice relentless. "Did she ever ask you about your work? Show interest in specific cases or clients?"

Jake hesitated, recalling their many conversations. "She was curious about my job, but nothing specific. Just general interest."

"Did she ever ask for sensitive information or access to your files?" another agent asked, her eyes narrowing as she scrutinized Jake's response.

Jake felt a surge of defensiveness. "No, never. Emily respected my work and never overstepped any boundaries."

The questions continued, each one more invasive than the last. The agents wanted to know everything—every detail about their relationship, every place they had visited together, every conversation they had ever had. Jake was asked to recount their weekend getaways in painstaking detail: the quaint countryside inn they frequented, the exact moments they shared by the lake, and the intimate conversations they had under the starlit sky.

"Tell us about your trips," Agent Collins prompted.

"We often went to a countryside inn," Jake began. "It was our escape from the city. We'd walk through the gardens, sit by the lake, and just talk for hours."

"What did you talk about during these trips?" another agent asked, leaning forward.

"Mostly personal stuff," Jake said. "Our dreams, our fears, and everything in between. She was charming, intelligent, and made me feel like the most important person in the world."

"Did she ever seem distracted or preoccupied?" an agent pressed.

"No, she was always present," Jake replied. "Engaged. We talked about our future, our plans. She never showed any signs of hiding something."

"Did she ever ask about your work in detail?" another agent inquired.

"She was curious about my job," Jake admitted, "but never pressed for specific details. It was more about showing interest in what I do."

"Did she ever give you any gifts or ask for favors?" the agent continued.

"We exchanged gifts, but nothing extravagant," Jake said, shaking his head. "She never asked for anything unusual."

The agents probed into the nuances of their discussions, whether she ever seemed unusually interested in his work or displayed any odd behavior.

"Did she ever ask for sensitive information or access to your files?" an agent asked, her eyes narrowing.

"No, never," Jake replied firmly. "Emily respected my work and never overstepped any boundaries."

"Did she ever receive any unusual phone calls or messages during your time together?" another agent asked.

"She got work calls, but she always said they were related to her job," Jake explained.

The agents listened intently, occasionally jotting down notes, their expressions revealing nothing but a relentless pursuit of the truth. Each answer Jake gave felt like another layer of his cherished memories being stripped away, leaving him feeling more vulnerable and exposed.

"When was the last time you saw her?" Agent Collins asked.

"Just a few days ago," Jake replied. "We spent the weekend together. Everything seemed normal."

"Did she say anything about her upcoming plans or travels?" the agent pressed.

"She mentioned another business trip," Jake said, trying to recall the details. "She didn't specify where."

The questioning went on for what felt like hours. The agents probed every aspect of their relationship, looking for any hint of espionage or suspicious behavior. Jake felt increasingly drained, each question stripping away another layer of the life he thought he knew. Finally, the interrogation ended. Jake was exhausted, emotionally drained by the relentless questioning and the realization that his entire relationship was under scrutiny.

As he stood to leave, Agent Collins handed him a card. "Mr. Jake, if you remember anything else or if Emily contacts you, please call us immediately."

Jake nodded, taking the card without a word. He walked out of the building, the cool evening air hitting his face as he stepped outside. He took a deep breath, trying to clear his mind. The reality of the situation was overwhelming, and he felt a profound sense of betrayal and loss.

As he made his way to his car, the events of the past few hours replayed in his mind. The woman he loved was now a wanted criminal, and he was caught in the middle of a nightmare. The weight of the situation pressed down on him, leaving him feeling hollow and confused.

His phone buzzed again, jolting him from his thoughts. He pulled it out, expecting another call from the FBI, but froze when he saw the name on the screen. The name "Emily" flashed in bold letters, and his heart pounded in his chest. He hesitated for a moment, his mind racing with conflicting emotions. Finally, he answered, his voice trembling.

A Plea for Help

Jake stood in the parking lot, his phone pressed to his ear, his mind a whirlwind of emotions. The voice on the other end of the line was unmistakable. It was Emily, sounding desperate and frightened.

"Jake, it's me," she said, her voice trembling. "I need your help."

"Emily, what's going on? They're saying you're a spy," Jake replied, trying to keep his voice calm despite the turmoil inside him. His hands shook, and he clenched his phone tighter to steady them.

"I'm being framed," Emily insisted, her voice urgent. "I need you to represent me. I want to come back to the USA and clear my name. I want to live a life with you."

Jake took a deep breath, his mind racing with conflicting thoughts. He wanted to believe her, to trust that the woman he loved was telling the truth. "Where are you?" he asked, his voice strained.

"I can't tell you that right now," Emily replied, her voice cracking. "But I trust you, Jake. Please, help me."

Jake's heart ached at the desperation in her voice. The woman he loved was in danger, and despite everything, he couldn't turn his back on her. "I'll do whatever it takes, Emily. Just come back safely," he said, his voice filled with determination.

"Thank you," she whispered, relief evident in her tone. "I knew I could count on you."

"Emily, I need more information. How can I help if I don't know where you are or what's happening?" Jake pressed, hoping to get some details.

"I can't risk telling you everything over the phone," Emily said. "It's not safe. But I promise, I'll explain everything when I see you."

"Alright," Jake agreed, though his mind was still filled with doubts and questions. "Just stay safe. We'll figure this out together."

"I will," Emily assured him. "I'll contact you soon with more details. Please, just trust me."

"I trust you," Jake said, though the words felt heavy with the weight of uncertainty. "Be careful, Emily."

The call ended, and Jake stood there for a moment, staring at his phone. The love of his life was accused of being a spy, and now she was asking for his help to clear her name. He knew the road ahead would be fraught with challenges and danger, but he couldn't abandon her.

As he drove home, his mind raced with thoughts of what to do next. He needed to prepare for the legal battle ahead, gather evidence, and find a way to prove Emily's innocence. But above all, he needed to confront his own doubts and fears, to find the strength to stand by the woman he loved despite the mounting evidence against her.

Jake knew he was stepping into uncharted territory, risking everything for a chance at the truth. But for Emily, he was willing to face it all. He just hoped that in the end, their love would be enough to see them through.

A New Mission

Over the next few days, Jake immersed himself in preparing for the most challenging case of his life. The weight of Emily's future pressed heavily on his shoulders, but his resolve remained unshaken. He spent countless hours in his office, surrounded by piles of documents, photographs, and evidence that could potentially clear her name.

Jake started by revisiting every detail Emily had shared with him, trying to piece together a coherent timeline that would support her claims of innocence. He reached out to old contacts in the legal field, seeking advice and guidance. Some were skeptical, but others offered their help, intrigued by the high-stakes nature of the case.

He began compiling a comprehensive dossier on Emily, meticulously documenting their relationship, her travels, and any connections she had to the espionage accusations. He reviewed phone records, financial statements, and any communication they had exchanged. His days blurred into nights as he worked tirelessly, driven by a mix of love and determination.

Despite the overwhelming evidence against her, Jake believed in Emily's innocence. He recalled their intimate conversations, her genuine laughter, and the way she had looked at him with trust and affection. These memories fueled his determination to prove her innocence and bring her back safely.

Jake knew that Emily's return to the USA was fraught with danger. The authorities would be on high alert, and any misstep could lead to her immediate arrest or worse. He coordinated with trusted allies to devise a plan for her safe return, considering every possible scenario and contingency.

He also prepared for the legal battle that awaited them. Jake knew that public opinion would be swayed by the media's portrayal of Emily as a spy. He needed to gather credible witnesses, experts, and anyone who could testify to her character and the improbability of her involvement in espionage.

One evening, Jake sat in his dimly lit office, surrounded by stacks of papers and files. He took a moment to reflect on the journey ahead. Their love had been tested by distance, secrecy, and now, a battle for justice. The road would be difficult, but his love for Emily gave him the strength to fight for her freedom.

As he reviewed the evidence for the hundredth time, his phone buzzed with a message from Emily. It was a short, cryptic note indicating she had made it to a safe location and was preparing for her return. Jake's heart swelled with a mixture of relief and anxiety.

"Be careful," he replied, knowing that every word they exchanged could be scrutinized. "We'll get through this together."

Their love had been forged in the fires of uncertainty and danger, but Jake was ready to face whatever came their way. He was driven by the hope of a future together, free from the shadows of the past. As he closed his eyes for a brief moment of rest, he visualized a life where they could finally be at peace, knowing that their bond had endured the ultimate test.

In the days that followed, Jake's preparations intensified. He met with private investigators, scrutinized every piece of evidence, and rehearsed his legal arguments. He knew that the coming battle would be grueling, but he was prepared to give everything he had to ensure Emily's freedom and their chance at a life together.

As the day of Emily's return approached, Jake felt a mix of anticipation and dread. The stakes were higher than ever, and failure was not an option. He stood by the window, looking out at the city lights, drawing strength from the love that had brought them this far.

"Emily," he whispered to himself, "we're going to make it. I promise."

With renewed determination, Jake returned to his desk, ready to face the challenges ahead. The mission was clear: to clear Emily's name and reclaim their future, no matter the cost.

Unraveling the Truth

As the days passed, Jake became more immersed in the details of Emily's case. The more he dug, the more uneasy he felt. He spent countless hours sifting through the mountains of documents and evidence that the FBI had compiled against her. But something didn't add up. The timelines, the connections—there were inconsistencies that gnawed at him, keeping him awake at night.

One evening, as Jake sat in his dimly lit office, surrounded by files, he noticed something peculiar. A set of dates in the FBI's timeline didn't match up with the ones Emily had given him. According to the documents, Emily had been in Europe on a specific date when she had told him she was in South America. The discrepancy was small, but it was enough to catch Jake's attention. Determined to get to the bottom of it, he began cross-referencing travel logs, bank statements, and any other records he could find.

Jake's background as a criminal lawyer had taught him to trust his instincts, and right now, they were telling him that something was seriously wrong. He reached out to some old contacts, leveraging his legal expertise and connections to gain access to classified information. Slowly but surely, a different picture of Emily began to emerge—one that didn't align with the woman he thought he knew.

One night, while sifting through a particularly old stack of documents, Jake found something that made his blood run cold. Tucked away in a file was a photograph of Emily with a man Jake didn't recognize. The photo was worn, the edges frayed, as if it had been handled many times. The date on the back indicated it had been taken several years before Jake and Emily had met. The man in the photograph was listed as a high-ranking officer in the German intelligence agency.

Jake's heart pounded in his chest as he stared at the photograph. Who was this man? And why was Emily with him? The questions swirled in Jake's mind, each one more troubling than the last. He knew he had to confront Emily about this, but he also knew that this conversation could change everything.

Taking a deep breath, Jake reached for his phone and contacted Emily through their secure communication channel. His hands trembled slightly as he waited for her to pick up.

"Jake?" Emily's voice came through the line, soft and familiar, yet tinged with apprehension.

"Emily," Jake began, trying to keep his voice steady, "I found something. A photograph of you with a German intelligence officer. What is this about?"

There was a long, tense pause on the other end of the line. Jake could almost hear Emily's mind racing as she tried to figure out how to respond.

"Jake," she finally said, her voice heavy with emotion, "I didn't want to involve you in this."

"Involve me in what, Emily?" Jake pressed, his frustration and confusion bubbling to the surface. "Who is this man? What are you hiding from me?"

"That man is my brother," Emily confessed, her voice barely above a whisper.

Jake felt as if the ground had shifted beneath him. "Your brother? Why didn't you tell me?"

"Because it's complicated," Emily replied, her tone pleading for understanding. "Klaus and I haven't been close for years. He's been involved in things that I wanted no part of. But recently, things have gotten out of control."

Jake took a moment to process what she was saying. "Why didn't you tell me any of this before? You knew how much I was risking for you, and yet you kept this from me?"

"I was trying to protect you," Emily said, her voice trembling. "I didn't want you to be dragged into my family's mess. But now it's too late. Klaus framed me to protect himself. He's the one who's been involved in espionage, not me. I've been trying to stop him, but he's always one step ahead."

Jake's mind raced as he tried to reconcile this new information with everything he knew—or thought he knew—about Emily. "So you're telling me that you've been framed by your own brother? And that's why the FBI is after you?"

"Yes," Emily replied, her voice filled with desperation. "I didn't know how to tell you, Jake. I was afraid you wouldn't believe me."

Jake closed his eyes, rubbing his temples as he felt the weight of the situation pressing down on him. "Emily, this changes everything. If what you're saying is true, we need to find a way to prove it. But you have to be honest with me from now on. No more secrets."

"I swear, Jake," Emily said, her voice breaking. "No more secrets. I'll tell you everything you need to know."

Jake took a deep breath, trying to steady himself. "Alright. We'll figure this out together. But you need to give me all the information you have on Klaus. If we're going to clear your name, we need to expose him."

"I will," Emily promised. "I'll send you everything I have. But please, Jake, be careful. Klaus is dangerous. He won't hesitate to hurt anyone who gets in his way."

Jake nodded, even though she couldn't see him. "I'll be careful. Just get me the information, and we'll take it from there."

As he ended the call, Jake felt a mix of emotions—relief that Emily had finally opened up to him, but also a deep sense of unease. The stakes had just been raised, and the path ahead was more treacherous than ever. But one thing was clear: if they were going to survive this, they would have to rely on each other like never before.

Trust on the Line

Jake and Emily had spent weeks working tirelessly, albeit from a distance. With Emily still in hiding, their communications were limited to secure channels, but they had managed to devise a plan to expose Klaus and clear her name. Jake had gathered all the evidence they needed—records, documents, and testimonies that could link Klaus to his crimes and exonerate Emily. They were close, so close, to finally ending the nightmare that had taken over their lives.

The plan was simple, yet dangerous. Emily would return to the USA, and together, they would hand over the evidence to the authorities. It was a risky move, but it was the only way to clear her name and bring

Klaus to justice. Jake had coordinated every detail, from her safe return to their meeting with a trusted contact within the FBI. Everything seemed to be falling into place.

As the day of Emily's return approached, Jake found himself on edge. He knew that once she set foot back in the country, everything would move quickly. There would be no room for errors. They had prepared for every possible scenario, but the weight of what they were about to do was heavy on Jake's shoulders.

Late one evening, just before Emily was scheduled to board the plane that would bring her back to the USA, Jake received a message on his phone. It was from an unknown number, and the content made his blood run cold.

"Be careful who you trust. Emily isn't who she claims to be."

Jake stared at the screen, his mind racing. Who could have sent this? What did it mean? The timing couldn't have been worse. Just when they were about to take the final step, doubt was suddenly cast over everything. He knew he had to confront Emily, but the very thought of it filled him with dread.

With a heavy heart, Jake reached out to Emily through their secure communication channel. The connection was brief, as it had to be for security reasons, but her voice came through clear, filled with the same determination that had kept them both going.

"Jake, everything is ready," Emily said, her voice steady. "I'm about to board the plane. We're almost there."

"Emily, wait," Jake said, trying to keep the tremor out of his voice. "I just received a message... an anonymous tip. It said I should be careful who I trust—that you're not who you claim to be."

There was a long pause on the other end. Jake could almost hear the wheels turning in Emily's mind as she processed what he had just said.

"Jake, you can't believe that," Emily finally replied, her voice tinged with desperation. "I've told you everything. We're in this together. Whoever sent that message is trying to tear us apart, to make you doubt me."

"Is there something else you're not telling me?" Jake asked, his voice filled with a mix of hope and fear. "Anything at all, Emily? We're so close... but I need to know I can trust you completely."

"Jake, I swear, I've told you everything," Emily said, her voice breaking slightly. "I don't know who sent that message, but you have to believe me. I'm the same person I've always been. You know me."

Jake wanted to believe her. He wanted to trust her with everything he had, but the message had planted a seed of doubt that he couldn't ignore. "I've risked everything for you, Emily," he said, his voice heavy with emotion. "My career, my freedom... my life. And now, just as we're about to finally get through this, I get this message. How can I ignore it?"

"Jake, please," Emily whispered, her voice filled with tears. "We've come too far to let doubt destroy us. I'm getting on that plane, and I'm coming back to you. We'll face this together, and we'll bring Klaus down. But you have to trust me."

Jake closed his eyes, taking a deep breath as he struggled with the decision before him. The stakes had never been higher, and one wrong move could cost them everything.

Finally, he made his choice. "Alright, Emily," he said softly. "I trust you."

"Thank you, Jake," Emily said, relief washing over her voice. "I knew I could count on you. I'll see you soon."

The connection ended, and Jake was left alone with his thoughts. He had made his decision, but the doubt still gnawed at him. As he waited for Emily's return, he could only hope that he hadn't made a fatal mistake.

As the hours passed, Jake sat in his office, going over the plan one last time. The clock ticked down to the moment when Emily would land, and everything would be set in motion. The truth would soon reveal itself, one way or another.

The Final Gambit

Jake knew that the time had come to take a calculated risk. The doubts, the fears, and the uncertainty all converged into a single, decisive moment. He had to confront Klaus directly, but he also needed to be smart about it. Any misstep could ruin everything, and he couldn't afford to lose.

He arranged a meeting with Klaus, carefully crafting a narrative that he hoped would lure the man into a false sense of security. Pretending to be disillusioned with Emily and willing to negotiate a deal, Jake made it clear that he was desperate to protect himself, even if it meant betraying her.

The location for the meeting was chosen with care—a quiet, upscale bar in a secluded part of town. It was the kind of place where deals were made in hushed tones, away from prying eyes. Jake arrived early, his nerves taut as he went over the plan in his mind. Hidden in the inner pocket of his jacket was a small, high-quality recording device. It was the key to the entire operation. If he could get Klaus to confess, it would be over.

Klaus arrived right on time, a sleek figure in an expensive suit. His demeanor was confident, almost arrogant, as he walked over to Jake's table. They exchanged polite greetings, though the tension between them was palpable.

"Jake," Klaus said smoothly as he took a seat across from him, "I have to admit, I was surprised when you reached out. I thought you were completely in Emily's camp."

Jake forced a tight smile, leaning forward slightly. "Things change," he replied, keeping his voice steady. "I have to look out for myself, Klaus. Emily's situation is... complicated, and I can't afford to go down with her."

Klaus studied him for a moment, his sharp eyes searching for any sign of deception. Jake met his gaze head-on, refusing to flinch. He had to sell this.

"So, what exactly are you proposing?" Klaus asked, his tone casual but with an undercurrent of suspicion.

Jake took a deep breath, choosing his words carefully. "I know Emily's innocent," he began, watching Klaus's reaction closely. "But that doesn't mean I'm willing to go down with her. If I can help you clear things up and make this all go away, I want something in return. Protection, assurances... something to make sure I come out of this unscathed."

Klaus raised an eyebrow, a slight smirk playing on his lips. "And what makes you think I can offer you that?"

"You and I both know the truth," Jake said, leaning in further, lowering his voice. "I know you framed her, Klaus. I'm not here to judge—just to survive. If you disappear with what you've taken and leave her out to dry, I need to make sure I'm not caught in the crossfire."

Klaus's expression didn't change, but there was a flicker of something in his eyes—interest, perhaps, or maybe calculation. He leaned back in his chair, considering Jake's words.

"And what do you expect from me in return?" Klaus asked, his tone still guarded.

"Simple," Jake replied, keeping his tone as neutral as possible. "I need your word that once this is over, I'm in the clear. No one comes after me, and I get to walk away from this mess. In exchange, I'll do what I can to help you... smooth things over."

For a moment, Klaus didn't say anything. The silence stretched between them, thick with tension. Then, slowly, Klaus nodded, a cold smile curling his lips.

"Alright, Jake," he said, his voice low and dangerous. "I can work with that. To be honest, framing Emily was the easiest way to get the heat off my back. She's the perfect scapegoat—close enough to me to make it believable, but far enough removed that I can slip away with what I've taken. And once I'm gone, no one will ever find me."

Jake felt a surge of vindication at Klaus's words, but he forced himself to remain calm, his expression carefully neutral. "And the stolen intelligence?" Jake asked, keeping the conversation going, hoping to get more on tape.

Klaus chuckled softly. "Let's just say it's going to be very profitable for me. Once I'm settled, I'll be living a life of luxury somewhere far from here, and no one will ever know where I went."

Jake nodded, as if considering Klaus's words. "And Emily?"

Klaus waved a hand dismissively. "Emily will take the fall, just as planned. The authorities will focus on her, and by the time they realize she's innocent, it'll be too late. I'll be long gone."

Jake's heart pounded in his chest, but he kept his face impassive. He had what he needed. Now, it was time to act.

"Alright," Jake said, standing up slowly. "I think we have an understanding."

Klaus nodded, standing up as well. "I'll be in touch," he said, extending his hand.

Jake shook his hand, suppressing the urge to grimace at the contact. "Looking forward to it."

As they walked out of the bar, Jake discreetly signaled the authorities who were waiting nearby. The moment Klaus stepped outside, he was surrounded by agents, their guns drawn and ready.

Klaus's eyes widened in shock as he realized what was happening. "What is this?" he snarled, struggling as the agents moved in to restrain him.

Jake stepped forward, his voice calm but filled with resolve. "This is the end of the line, Klaus. You're under arrest for espionage, framing an innocent person, and countless other crimes. The evidence is all on tape."

Klaus glared at Jake, fury and betrayal etched on his face. "You think this changes anything? You're making a mistake, Jake."

"No," Jake replied, his voice firm. "The only mistake was thinking you could get away with it."

As the authorities led Klaus away, Jake felt a wave of relief wash over him. The recording was everything they needed to clear Emily's name. The nightmare was finally over.

But as he watched Klaus being taken into custody, a lingering sense of unease remained. The battle might be won, but the war was far from over. The truth had come to light, but at what cost?

The Calm Before the Storm

With Klaus in custody and the evidence submitted, Jake felt a sense of closure beginning to take hold. The months of tension, fear, and uncertainty seemed to melt away as the authorities lauded him for his bravery and meticulous work. It felt good to be recognized, but what mattered most was that Emily's name had been cleared. The truth about Klaus's involvement became widely known, and the narrative quickly shifted from suspicion to admiration for Jake's role in uncovering the conspiracy.

Jake and Emily were finally able to breathe easier. Emily returned to the USA, and they spent several quiet days together, trying to rebuild their lives after the storm. They retreated to Jake's home, where they found solace in the mundane—cooking meals together, taking long walks, and enjoying simple conversations about everything except the recent turmoil.

But even in those moments of peace, something gnawed at Jake. He couldn't shake the feeling that something was still off. Emily's behavior had shifted subtly. She was still the Emily he knew, but there was a guardedness to her now, a calculation in her actions that hadn't been there before.

One evening, as they sat on the couch watching a movie, Jake noticed how Emily seemed slightly distant. She was there, but her mind was somewhere else, her eyes flickering with thoughts she wasn't sharing.

"You okay?" Jake asked, reaching out to take her hand.

Emily smiled at him, but it didn't quite reach her eyes. "Yeah, I'm fine," she replied, giving his hand a reassuring squeeze. "Just tired, I guess. It's been a lot to process."

Jake nodded, trying to dismiss the unease that crept up his spine. "I get that. We've been through hell and back. It's going to take time to get back to normal."

"Normal," Emily echoed, almost wistfully. "Yeah, that sounds nice."

Jake searched her face, looking for any sign that she was hiding something, but she seemed genuine enough. Still, the doubt in his mind grew stronger each day. He wanted to trust her, to believe that they could move on, but the small inconsistencies in her behavior were hard to ignore.

A few days later, Jake found himself in the kitchen, making coffee while Emily was upstairs. He glanced out the window, watching the world go by, and couldn't help but think about how different things had been just a few weeks ago. They had been living in constant fear, but now that it was over, why couldn't he fully relax?

As he pondered this, Jake's phone buzzed on the counter. He picked it up, expecting a routine message, but his breath caught when he saw the name of the sender—Agent Collins, the FBI contact who had been involved in the operation to capture Klaus.

The message was short, but it sent a shiver down Jake's spine: *"We need to talk. There's something you should know."*

Jake stared at the screen, his heart pounding. What could this be about? He had thought everything was wrapped up, that the danger had passed. But now, with just a few words, that fragile sense of security was shattered.

"Jake?" Emily's voice called from the stairs, pulling him out of his thoughts.

"Yeah?" Jake replied, trying to keep his voice steady as he slid the phone back into his pocket.

"Everything okay?" she asked, appearing at the bottom of the stairs with a curious look.

Jake forced a smile. "Yeah, just thinking about heading into town later. Want to come?"

Emily hesitated for a moment before nodding. "Sure, that sounds nice."

As they prepared to go out, Jake's mind raced with possibilities. What could Agent Collins have to say that was so important? And why did it feel like this was only the beginning of something even more dangerous?

Once they were in the car, Jake drove in silence, his thoughts consumed by the cryptic message. He knew he needed to meet with Agent Collins, but he couldn't let Emily know just yet. Not until he had more information.

"Jake, are you sure everything's okay?" Emily asked again, glancing at him as they drove.

"Yeah, just got a lot on my mind," Jake replied, forcing another smile. "But I'm fine, really."

Emily studied him for a moment before nodding. "Alright. Just let me know if you need to talk about anything."

"Will do," Jake said, his grip tightening on the steering wheel. He couldn't shake the feeling that everything was about to change once more, and not for the better.

When they returned home later that evening, Jake waited until Emily was in the shower before stepping out onto the porch to make a call. He dialed Agent Collins, his heart pounding as the phone rang.

"Collins," the agent answered, his voice brisk and professional.

"It's Jake," he said quietly, glancing back at the house to make sure Emily wasn't within earshot. "I got your message. What's going on?"

There was a pause on the other end, and Jake could almost hear the tension in the agent's voice. "Jake, I need you to listen carefully. We've been reviewing the case, going through all the evidence again, and something's come up."

Jake felt a cold knot of fear tighten in his chest. "What is it?"

"There's something off about Klaus's confession," Collins continued. "We think he might have been coerced, or worse, that someone else was pulling the strings. I need you to come in. There's more you need to know, but we can't discuss it over the phone."

Jake's mind raced as he processed the information. "You think someone else was involved? Who?"

"I can't say for sure yet," Collins replied, his voice grave. "But you need to be careful, Jake. This isn't over."

Jake closed his eyes, feeling the weight of the situation pressing down on him. "I'll be there tomorrow," he said, his voice steady despite the turmoil inside him.

"Good. And Jake... be careful who you trust," Collins warned before ending the call.

As Jake stood on the porch, the cool night air brushing against his skin, he realized that the nightmare wasn't over after all. The truth was still out there, buried beneath layers of deception and lies. And now, he had to find it—before it destroyed him.

When he walked back into the house, Emily was in the kitchen, drying her hair with a towel. She smiled at him, but Jake could see the flicker of something else in her eyes—something that made his blood run cold.

"Everything alright?" she asked, her voice light and casual.

"Yeah," Jake replied, forcing a smile of his own. "Everything's fine."

But he knew that wasn't true. The storm was far from over, and the real battle was just beginning.

Unveiling the Deception

Jake drove through the dimly lit streets, his thoughts racing as he approached the secluded location where he was supposed to meet his FBI contact. The message he had received had been cryptic, but the urgency in Agent Collins's voice had been unmistakable. He knew that whatever he was about to hear would change everything.

The meeting point was a small, nondescript café on the outskirts of town. It was the kind of place where people could talk without being overheard, where secrets were shared and deals were made in hushed tones. Jake parked his car around the corner and walked the rest of the way, his heart pounding in his chest.

When he entered the café, he saw Agent Collins sitting in a back booth, his expression tense and his posture rigid. The agent looked up as Jake approached, giving him a curt nod.

"Jake," Collins greeted him, his voice low and serious.

"Collins," Jake replied, sliding into the seat across from him. "What's going on? You said there was something I needed to know."

Collins glanced around the nearly empty café before leaning in, his voice barely above a whisper. "We've been reviewing the case," he began, his tone heavy with the weight of what he was about to reveal. "There's something about Klaus's confession that doesn't add up."

Jake frowned, confusion and disbelief washing over him. "What do you mean? He confessed to everything."

"That's just it," Collins said, shaking his head. "We believe Klaus might have been coerced."

Jake stared at him, trying to process the information. "Coerced? By who?"

Collins hesitated, his eyes flicking up to meet Jake's. "We believe someone else was pulling the strings, and Klaus was taking the fall to protect them."

Jake's heart skipped a beat, a cold dread settling in his stomach. "Who?" he asked, his voice barely a whisper.

"Emily," Collins said, the name hanging in the air like a dark cloud.

"Emily?" Jake repeated, his voice cracking as the realization hit him like a freight train. The woman he had loved, the woman he had fought to protect, had been the mastermind all along?

Collins nodded grimly. "We found new evidence—a hidden network of communications and payments that trace back to her. It looks like she orchestrated everything, using Klaus as a pawn to cover her tracks."

Jake's mind reeled. He had put everything on the line to clear Emily's name, and now he was faced with the possibility that she had played him all along. He felt sick to his stomach, the room spinning around him as he tried to make sense of what he was hearing.

"But why would Klaus confess?" Jake asked, desperation lacing his voice. "Why would he take the fall if Emily was the real culprit?"

Collins sighed, leaning back in his seat. "We believe Klaus may have confessed because he thought it was the only way to protect someone— his sister. He was loyal to her until the end."

Jake's hands shook as he processed the information. "So, she's been lying to me this whole time? What about the evidence we found against Klaus?"

"It was planted," Collins confirmed, his voice steady but filled with a quiet fury. "Emily has been manipulating events from the very begin- ning, making sure she always stayed one step ahead. She used you, Jake, to get exactly what she wanted."

Jake felt the blood drain from his face as the full weight of the betrayal settled over him. Emily had played him from the start, weaving a web of lies and deceit that had ensnared him completely. He had been nothing more than a pawn in her game, a tool she had used to achieve her goals.

"I don't believe it," Jake said, his voice trembling. "She... she wouldn't do that. Not after everything we've been through."

Collins's expression softened slightly, but his eyes were still hard. "Jake, I know this is hard to hear, but you need to face the truth. Emily is dangerous. She's been playing this game for a long time, and she's very good at it."

Jake shook his head, his mind racing as he tried to piece together the events of the past few months. Every conversation, every interaction with Emily now seemed tainted, twisted by the knowledge that she had been deceiving him all along.

"What do we do now?" Jake asked, his voice hollow.

"We need to bring her in," Collins said firmly. "We have enough evidence to arrest her, but we need your help to make it happen. You're the only one who can get close enough to her."

Jake's heart sank as he realized what Collins was asking of him. He had loved Emily, had trusted her with everything he had, and now he was being asked to betray her in return. But what choice did he have? If what Collins was saying was true, then Emily was a threat, not just to him, but to everyone around her.

"Alright," Jake said, his voice filled with resolve. "I'll do it. I'll help you bring her in."

Collins nodded, his expression grave. "Thank you, Jake. I know this isn't easy, but it's the right thing to do."

Jake forced himself to nod, even though every fiber of his being wanted to scream. The woman he had loved was a lie, a carefully constructed facade designed to manipulate and control him. And now, he had to be the one to bring her down.

As they left the café, Jake felt a heavy weight settle on his shoulders. The truth had been revealed, but it had come at a terrible cost. The road ahead would be difficult, but there was no turning back now. The only thing he could do was move forward and hope that, in the end, justice would prevail.

But as he drove home, the doubt in his mind only grew stronger. How could he have been so blind? How could he have let himself be deceived so completely? And, most importantly, what would he do when the time came to confront Emily?

When Jake arrived home, Emily was waiting for him, her eyes filled with concern as she asked, "Jake, is everything alright?"

Jake looked at her, seeing her now through a lens of suspicion and betrayal. "Yeah," he said, forcing a smile. "Everything's fine."

But he knew it wasn't. The truth had shattered everything he thought he knew, and the final confrontation was looming on the horizon. The woman he had once loved was now his enemy, and soon, he would have to face her with the knowledge of the lies she had woven around him.

The Final Deception

Jake returned home, his mind swirling with a storm of emotions—anger, betrayal, disbelief. The revelation from Agent Collins had shattered everything he thought he knew. Emily, the woman he had loved and fought for, was a fraud. The knowledge weighed heavily on him as he approached the door to his apartment.

When he walked inside, the familiar surroundings felt foreign, tainted by the truth he had uncovered. Emily was waiting for him, standing near the kitchen with a glass of wine in her hand. Her posture was relaxed, almost casual, but her expression was unreadable. She looked up as he entered, her voice soft, almost too soft.

"Jake," she said, her tone carefully measured. "What's wrong?"

Jake's heart pounded as he looked at her, seeing her now in a completely different light. The woman he had trusted, who had shared his life, was nothing more than a master manipulator. "You knew, didn't you?" he accused, his voice trembling with a mixture of anger and hurt. "You knew Klaus would confess, and you let him take the fall."

Emily didn't deny it. Instead, she set down her glass with a calm, almost practiced motion, and met Jake's gaze head-on. "I did what I had to do," she replied, her voice cold and detached. "Klaus was always a liability. He was reckless, and he would have gotten us both killed."

Jake felt his anger flare, the betrayal cutting deep. "And what about me?" he demanded, his voice rising. "Was I just a pawn too? Did you ever care about me at all?"

For a moment, Emily's expression softened, but there was still a hard edge in her eyes. "Jake, I did care about you," she admitted, taking a small step closer. "I still do. But this is bigger than you or me. I couldn't let everything I've worked for fall apart because of Klaus's incompetence."

Jake's fists clenched at his sides, his mind racing. "So, you used me," he said, the realization hitting him with full force. "You manipulated me into helping you, knowing full well that you were the real spy all along."

Emily didn't flinch. Instead, she moved even closer, her gaze intense and unyielding. "Jake, I never wanted to hurt you," she said, her voice low and urgent. "But you have to understand—I'm in too deep. There's no turning back now. I need you to trust me one last time."

Jake shook his head, the betrayal cutting him deeper than any wound ever could. "How can I trust you after everything?" he asked, his voice filled with pain. "You've lied to me, used me, and now you expect me to just go along with whatever you're planning next?"

Emily's eyes hardened again, her voice dropping to a dangerous whisper. "If you don't help me, Jake, you'll be the one going down for this," she warned, her tone cold and calculating. "I have enough evidence to implicate you in everything we've done. If you want to survive, you'll need to come with me."

Jake stared at her, realizing the full extent of her manipulation. She had always been a step ahead, always in control. Now, he was faced with an impossible choice—run with her and become complicit in her crimes, or stay and risk losing everything, including his freedom.

"Emily, you've destroyed everything," Jake said, his voice filled with a mix of sadness and anger. "But I won't go down with you."

For a brief moment, something like regret flickered in Emily's eyes, but it was quickly replaced by the same cold resolve. "Then this is good-bye, Jake," she said, her voice final.

Without another word, Emily turned and walked out the door, leaving Jake standing in the wreckage of their relationship. The sound of the door closing echoed in the now-empty apartment, a final punctuation mark on the end of what they had shared. Jake felt a crushing sense of loss and betrayal. The woman he had loved was gone, and in her place was a criminal mastermind who had played him from the very beginning.

Jake stood frozen in place for what felt like an eternity, the reality of what had just happened slowly sinking in. The person he thought he knew had been nothing more than an illusion, a carefully crafted persona designed to manipulate him. And now, she was gone, leaving him to pick up the pieces of his shattered life.

He knew he had to act fast. The authorities needed to know the truth, and he had to ensure that Emily didn't get away. With a heavy heart, Jake contacted Agent Collins, providing him with the new information he had learned. The call was brief, but the urgency in Jake's voice was unmistakable. Collins assured him that a manhunt would be launched to track down Emily, but Jake knew deep down that she was already gone—disappeared without a trace, just as Klaus had planned to do.

As Jake sat in his now-empty apartment, the weight of the betrayal settled over him like a heavy blanket. He had been outsmarted, betrayed, and left to pick up the pieces of a life that would never be the same. The truth had finally been revealed, but the cost had been everything he held dear.

The woman he had once loved was now a ghost, a shadow that haunted his every thought. And as the days passed, Jake found himself grappling with a new reality—one in which trust was a fragile thing, easily shattered and impossible to fully rebuild. The nightmare was over, but the scars it left behind would remain with him forever.

The Ghosts That Remain

Months had passed since Emily had vanished from Jake's life, but the impact of her betrayal lingered like a shadow over everything he did. He had tried to move on, to rebuild the pieces of his shattered world, but some things couldn't be repaired. The weight of what had happened bore down on him every day, reminding him of how close he had come to losing everything.

Jake had left his law practice behind, unable to return to the life he had once known. The office that had been his second home felt tainted now, a place where he had unknowingly fought for a lie. His colleagues had expressed their shock and sympathy, but Jake could see the unspoken question in their eyes—how could he have been so blind?

He had sold his apartment, too, moving to a small, quiet town where he could be anonymous. The city that had once held so much promise now felt like a graveyard of memories, filled with too many ghosts. In his new home, he spent his days doing menial work, tasks that required little thought, allowing his mind to drift away from the pain.

One evening, as Jake sat on the porch of his modest house, a glass of whiskey in hand, he received a call from Agent Collins. It had been months since they last spoke, the investigation into Emily's disappearance having gone cold.

"Jake," Collins said, his voice tinged with something Jake couldn't quite place—regret, perhaps, or maybe frustration. "Just wanted to check in. How are you holding up?"

Jake took a long sip of his drink before replying. "I'm surviving," he said, his voice hollow. "But I'm not sure that's enough."

Collins sighed on the other end of the line. "I get it. We did everything we could, but she's a ghost now. No trace, no sightings. It's like she never existed."

Jake nodded, even though Collins couldn't see him. "That's what she does best, isn't it? Disappears when things get too hot."

"Yeah," Collins agreed, a note of bitterness creeping into his voice. "But don't think for a second that we're giving up. We'll find her. It's just a matter of time."

Jake wasn't so sure. Emily had always been several steps ahead, always in control. The thought that she was out there, somewhere, continuing her work, manipulating others as she had manipulated him, made his skin crawl.

"Do you think she's still in the game?" Jake asked, the question slipping out before he could stop it.

Collins was silent for a moment, as if considering how much to say. "If I had to guess, yeah," he finally admitted. "People like her don't just walk away. She's probably already moved on to her next mark, setting up another play."

Jake felt a cold knot tighten in his chest. The idea of Emily out there, ruining lives, made him want to scream, to punch something, to take action. But what could he do? He had already lost everything in the fight to expose her, and now he was left with nothing but the bitter taste of defeat.

"Jake," Collins said softly, his tone shifting to one of genuine concern. "You did everything you could. You were a victim, just like the rest of us. Don't let her ruin what's left of your life. Move on, find peace. Don't let her win."

Jake closed his eyes, taking a deep breath as he tried to let Collins's words sink in. "I appreciate it, Collins," he said, though he wasn't sure he believed it. "But I'm not sure I know how to do that."

"You will," Collins replied, his voice firm. "It just takes time."

After they hung up, Jake sat there, staring out into the twilight, feeling more lost than ever. The sun was setting, casting long shadows across the yard, and as the darkness crept in, Jake felt the weight of his solitude.

The authorities had closed the case on Emily, but she had never been found. She had vanished into the shadows, leaving behind only the memory of the woman Jake had once loved. But Jake knew the truth. Emily was out there, somewhere, continuing her work, playing her games, and manipulating those who crossed her path. And Jake was left to wonder if he would ever be free of the ghost of the woman who had nearly destroyed him.

He thought about the man he had been before Emily entered his life—confident, driven, passionate about his work. That man was gone now, replaced by someone who saw the world through a lens of distrust and cynicism. Jake had learned the hard way that the truth was a double-edged sword. It had brought him clarity, but it had also shattered his world.

In the end, Jake realized that the only thing he could do now was move forward, knowing that he had survived, even if it had cost him everything he once believed in. He would never be the same, and maybe that was the hardest truth of all to accept.

As the last rays of sunlight faded, Jake downed the rest of his whiskey and stood up. He walked inside, closing the door behind him, and locked it tight. The world outside was filled with shadows, but Jake was done living in fear of them. He had faced the darkness and come out the other side—scarred, yes, but still standing.

Tomorrow was a new day, and for the first time in a long while, Jake allowed himself to believe that maybe, just maybe, he could find a way to live again.

www.ingramcontent.com/pod-product-compliance
Lightning Source LLC
Chambersburg PA
CBHW071247130726
47998CB00003B/1078